Blowin' in the Wind

LYRICS BY
Bob Dylan

ILLUSTRATIONS BY
Jon J Muth

STERLING CHILDREN'S BOOKS
New York

How many roads
     must a man walk down
Before you call
     him a man?

How many seas
  must the white dove sail
Before she sleeps
  in the sand?

Yes, 'n' how many times
        must the cannonballs fly
Before they're
        forever banned?

The answer, my friend,
      is blowin' in the wind
The answer is
      blowin' in the wind

Yes, 'n' how many years
can a mountain exist
Before it is washed
to the sea?

Yes, 'n' how many years
        can some people exist
    Before they're allowed
            to be free?

Yes, 'n' how many times
     can a man turn his head
And pretend that he
     just doesn't see?

The answer, my friend,
    is blowin' in the wind
The answer is
    blowin' in the wind

Yes, 'n' how many times
must a man look up
Before he can
see the sky?

Yes, 'n' how many ears
must one man have
Before he can
hear people cry?

Yes, 'n' how many deaths
        will it take till he knows
That too many
        people have died?

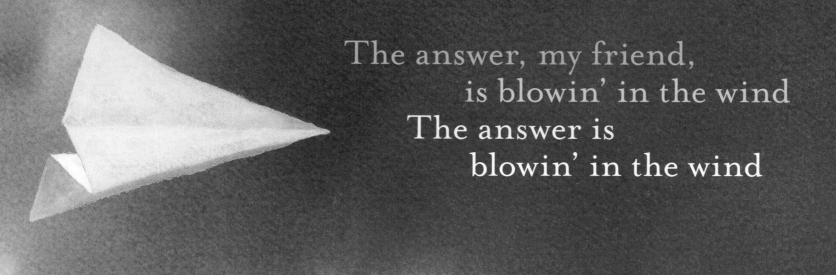

The answer, my friend,
  is blowin' in the wind
The answer is
  blowin' in the wind

A Note from Artist JON J MUTH

I remember walking down the street in 1972 and holding a transistor radio up to my ear. I was a twelve-year-old imagining the adult I wanted to be. Then I heard, "The answer, my friend, is blowin' in the wind." It pulled me out of my imaginings. At that moment I felt nudged forward and backward in time, like the lyrics: naive and knowing . . . eager and wise . . . old and young. Bob Dylan has given us an amazing number of songs that have made people all over the world feel this way.

No matter how many maps we give them, our children will never know where they are until they walk the territory. It's for each of us to do our own learning.

In order to make "Blowin' in the Wind" into a book for young readers, I thought the "answer" in the wind might be on a sheet of paper, and made into a paper airplane. This airplane would be found in places which reflect the lyrics of the song. It's a visual metaphor, maybe the way a child would see it.

The beauty of this song is that, while Dylan wrote it at a seminal moment, its sentiment is universal and timeless. Just as each of the children in my illustrations has his or her own paper airplane, each of us knows what needs to be done in our worlds. The song speaks to a truth found in us all. When we approach life with an open and dedicated mind and heart, what do we experience? We learn that we are striving for the same things—love, honesty, justice. We find these are actions, not wishes or longings. Freedom and joy are not care-free. Escape from the burdens of life isn't freedom. Freedom is full of care for everything. That means we must be a part of what all people want for themselves and for humanity.

The doors of the heart will then be thrown open to wind from every direction.

A Note from GREIL MARCUS,
Music Historian and Author of *Mystery Train: Images of America in Rock 'n' Roll Music*

The words you've just heard, the pictures you've looked at—the story they tell—come from a song written almost fifty years ago by a singer named Bob Dylan: a song called "Blowin' in the Wind."

Bob Dylan is still traveling all over the world and singing this song. Almost any night, he might be in your town, playing his music. People of all ages are always there to watch and listen. But it is not only Dylan who sings "Blowin' in the Wind." Hundreds of others have recorded their own versions of the song—country singers, soul singers, jazz musicians, gospel choirs. People have sung it on bus trips, on hikes, sitting around campfires, in churches, and in schools. And when Dylan sings the song, it is almost always different. Sometimes it is a hopeful song. Sometimes it is full of doubt.

"Blowin' in the Wind" asks questions. When there is trouble in the world, in our own towns, in our own families, why can't we admit that something is wrong, and try to do something about it? Why are some citizens treated unfairly? Why do some people think they are better than others? Why do we fight each other? But when Bob Dylan first recorded "Blowin' in the Wind" in 1963, many people believed he was singing about one thing more than anything else.

In the United States fifty years ago, many people were not treated like real Americans. In parts of our country, those with dark skin were not allowed to live where they wanted to live. They were not allowed to vote for president. They were not allowed to eat in restaurants. They were not allowed in movie theaters. They were not free.

When Bob Dylan first asked, "How many roads must a man walk down before you call him a man?" it was this unfair America that many people heard Dylan singing about. And because the injustice in his song was so big, and so much a part of life, it made every other question he was asking feel just as big.

The United States is a very different place today. It is not perfect. It still does not keep all of its promises. But because many men and women worked hard to answer the kinds of questions Bob Dylan asked in his song, our country is far more free than it was when "Blowin' in the Wind" was written. So why are we still singing it? The song doesn't say anything about people with dark skin. It doesn't mention any particular war. But Bob Dylan was able to write about certain ideas using words that could be interpreted to mean many other things, too. There are people in his song. There are birds. There are mountains. There is the ocean. There is wind. And there are questions. Why is the world the way it is? Why do we have war, cruelty, and hate? Will this ever change?

So today, whenever people feel that they are not free. . .
Whenever they feel they are being treated unfairly. . .
Whenever they know others only see what they look like, and not who they really are. . .
Whenever their lives are hurt or even destroyed by war or poverty. . .
They can listen to "Blowin' in the Wind." They can say:
Yes. I am in that song. That song is about me, too.

For Bonnie
—J J M

STERLING CHILDREN'S BOOKS
New York

An Imprint of Sterling Publishing
387 Park Avenue South
New York, NY 10016

Blowin' in the Wind
Words and Music by Bob Dylan
Copyright © 1962 by Warner Bros. Inc.;
renewed 1990 by Special Rider Music
Illustrations © 2011 by Jon J Muth
Art Direction by Jeff Batzli
Designed by Merideth Harte

The artwork for this book was prepared using watercolor paints.

ISBN 978-1-4027-8002-8

Distributed in Canada by Sterling Publishing
c/o Canadian Manda Group, 165 Dufferin Street
Toronto, Ontario, Canada M6K 3H6
Distributed in the United Kingdom by GMC Distribution Services
Castle Place, 166 High Street, Lewes, East Sussex, England BN7 1XU

For information about custom editions, special sales, and premium and corporate purchases,
please contact Sterling Special Sales at 800-805-5489 or specialsales@sterlingpublishing.com.

Manufactured in China
Lot #:
2 4 6 8 10 9 7 5 3 1
09/11

www.sterlingpublishing.com/kids